CW00859065

Toucan Jan ©

LIFE IN THE ISLANDS
WRITTEN BY
BRENDA PANDER-STOWE

ILLUSTRATED BY
DAVID THRASHER

Toucan Jan

is dedicated to our children

Nicolette and Jaeda

and

Damian and Ariel
Sunny and Ping

May you always
keep a little of the islands in your heart
turn your face to the sun
and let the blues of the ocean
soothe your soul.

Copyright © 2022 Brenda Pander-Stowe, Author, David Thrasher, Artist.

Published by Classic Concepts: classic@sasktel.net

ISBN: 978-0-9736189-2-1

Get up Toucan Jan
and don't delay.
We have friends to meet
down in the bay.

Let's join Toucan Jan stopping in to see Nicolette, Dexter & Mumbles the monkey.

We're all different
in a special way,
visit our island
and spend the whole day.

We'll play on the beach
and dig in the sand,
building a castle
that's really quite grand.

Swim fast in the sea
and catch a big wave.

Mumbles won't join in,
he's not very brave.

Today Hee Haw
will be our guide
to a beautiful rain forest
in the hills nearby.

Rain forests are cool
and always quite green,
lots of small creatures
can't even be seen.

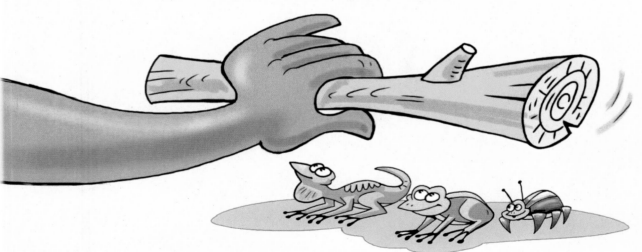

Like gecko lizards
and cute coqui frogs,
a big black beetle hides
under a log.

All island parrots
are most special birds.
They are rarely seen
but quite often heard!

Mumbles is having
a wonderful time
as he swings along
reaching vine to vine.

A waterfall runs
by the riverside,

big plants like these
make a great place to hide.

Leaving the forest
for another day,
hop on old Hee Haw
and we're on our way.

Riding down the hillside
singing silly songs,
Hee Haw starts laughing
and gets the words wrong.

Down in the valley
we stop for a rest,
a coconut drink
is really the best.

Toucan Jan loves fruit!
"Pass the mango please."
See how bananas grow
upside down on trees.

Tropical flowers
add joy to our day
painting the landscape
a dazzling display.

Beneath a huge tree
Nicolette spots sheep.
When she looks closer
there's Dexter asleep.

We'll rent a small boat
before the day ends
to travel nearby
and visit some friends.

Lots of baby fish
are born in the sea,
growing up safely
by the mangrove tree.

Lobsters and turtles
and sea birds that roam

nest in the mangroves
and call it their home.

Toucan Jan's best friends
would just like to say
"Thanks for visiting
our island today."

Brenda and David both lived in the British Virgin Islands and combined their experiences of island life and individual skills to create the Toucan Jan series.

Brenda Pander-Stowe has written a rollicking series of four rhyming books starting with the adventures of **"Toucan Jan Life in the Islands."**

Her writing portfolio is varied from tourism, tall ships and island sights, three hardcover destination books as well as a middle grade and women's fiction novel.

Toucan Jan and Friends are very close to her heart and she looks forward to taking readers along with them as they explore **Life in the Islands.**

Brenda resides in a small lakeside town in Canada, but a piece of her heart will always be in the Caribbean. She is married with two children and has many favourite kids.

David Thrasher is an international artist best know for his work in the animation industry from 1975-2003 where he worked as an Animator, Layout Director and finally a Storyboard Artist. His animation credits with Disney, Nelvana, Nickelodean, M.G.M., D.I.C., Tony Collingwood among others can be viewed at IMDb.com/David Thrasher/Animation.

Mr. Thrasher additionally established Caribbean Landscapes Art Gallery from 2003-2009 where he produced two hundred acrylic canvases of the local scenery while teaching Art, which he continues to the present.

David spends most of his time as a professional children's book illustrator and Art teacher in Canada, the British Virgin Islands and Thailand.

We look forward to hearing from readers of all ages.

Made in the USA
Columbia, SC
25 November 2022